Noah
and the
Space Ark

by Laura Cecil
illustrated by Emma Chichester Clark

Carolrhoda Books, Inc./Minneapolis

Many, many years from now, Earth was very crowded. It was crammed with people, buildings, machines, and spaceships. There were no forests or big animals left: no elephants, rhinos, giraffes, or tigers.

There was only room for small animals.
They all lived in a park, where the last
trees and flowers grew.

The park was taken care of by Noah and
Mrs. Noah, with the help of their three sons,
Ham, Shem, and Japhet, and their families.

Every day, Noah cared for the plants and trees.
All the animals looked forward to his visits.

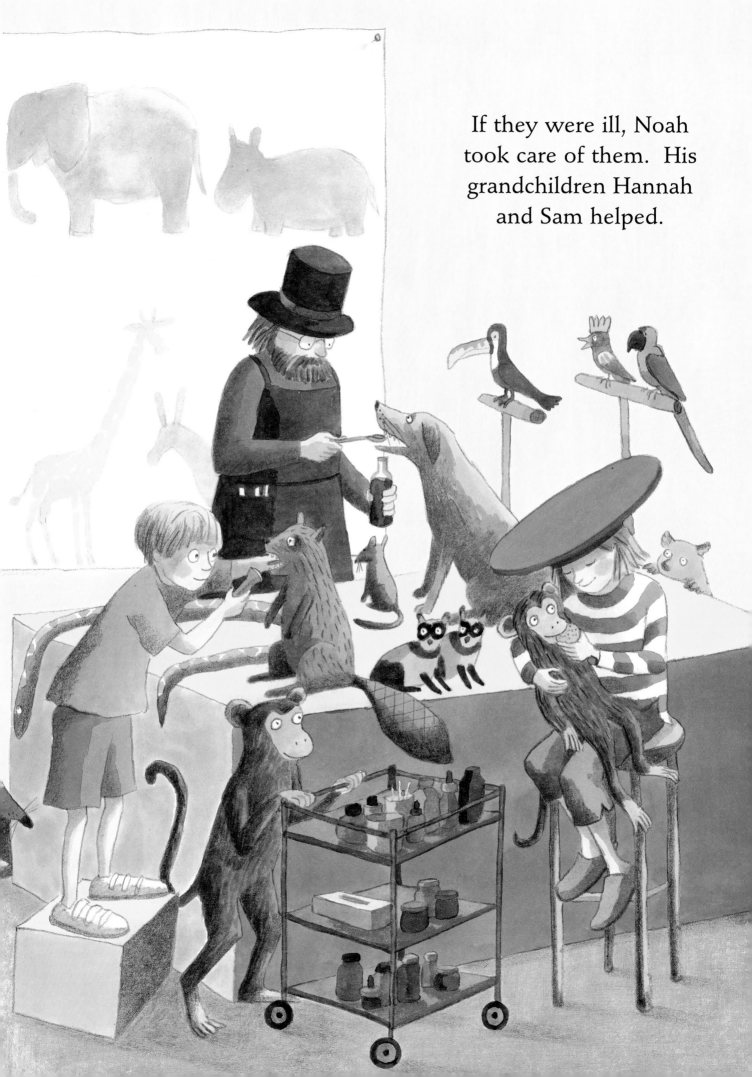

If they were ill, Noah took care of them. His grandchildren Hannah and Sam helped.

Then one year no rain fell. The sky was dark and smoky. The trees and plants drooped and would not grow, and the animals could not find enough to eat.

The next year there was still no rain. It grew stiflingly hot. One morning, Noah found a little bird gasping for breath.

The next day he found more sick animals.

Noah called the family together. "This is a warning,"
he said. "We cannot stay on Earth.
We must build a spaceship and find a new planet to live on."
"We must take the animals!" cried Sam and Hannah.
"Of course," said Mrs. Noah, "and we'll take plants and seeds, too."

So they went to the Build-It-Yourself superstore. Noah bought a rocket and a make-your-own spaceship kit.

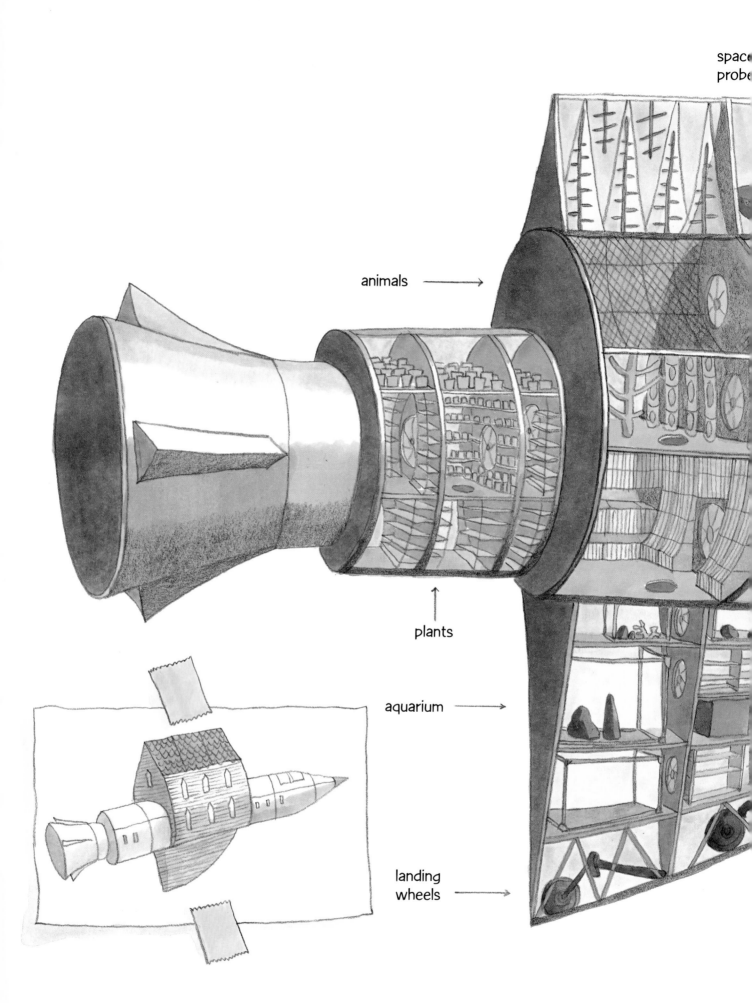

space
probe

animals →

plants ↑

aquarium →

landing
wheels →

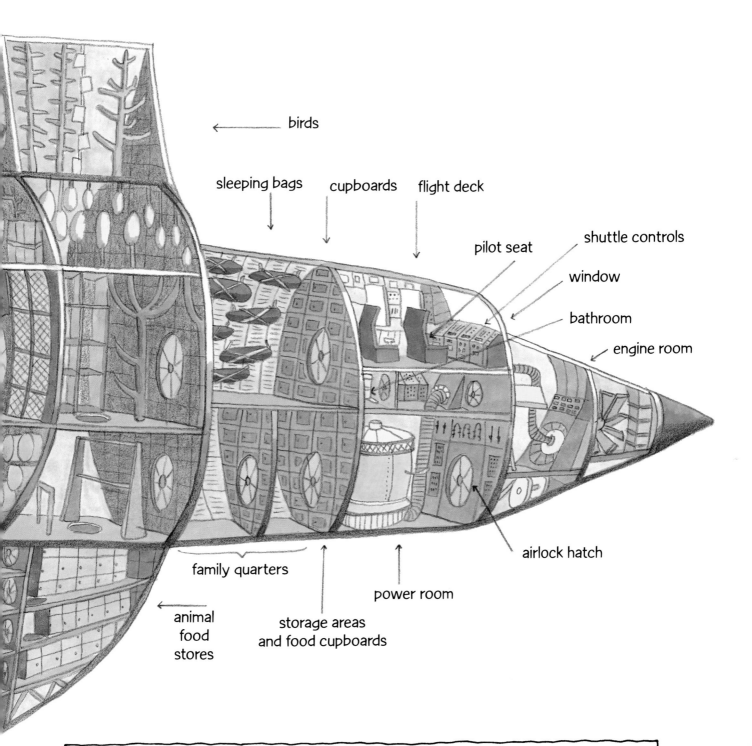

birds ←

sleeping bags   cupboards   flight deck

pilot seat

shuttle controls

window

bathroom

engine room

airlock hatch

family quarters

power room

animal food stores ←

storage areas and food cupboards

Noah called his creation the Space Ark. It was well planned. The small section at the front was for Noah's family. The middle section was for the animals, and the plants would be stored at the back.

Mrs. Noah prepared the plants
and trees for the journey.

When people heard about the Space Ark,
they crowded around to take a look.

Noah was interviewed on television. Everyone laughed when he told them why he was building the Space Ark.

But day after day, it grew warmer and warmer and the air grew thicker and smokier.

By the time the Space Ark was ready, it was unbearably hot and hard to breathe. "We must leave now!" cried Noah. "Go and find all the animals and get them on board quickly!"

Some of the animals came at once,

but some were asleep.

Others hid in unexpected places.

At last they all climbed aboard, two by two.

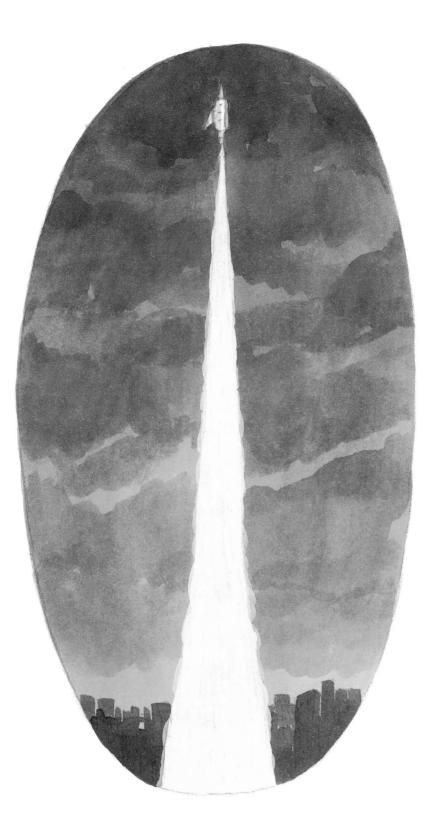

Noah counted: "Ten, nine, eight, seven, six, five, four, three, two, one, LIFT OFF!"

The rocket engines fired up with a roar. Then the Space Ark vanished into the sky.

When Sam and Hannah looked out, they could see Earth.
It glowed red with thick clouds of gas drifting around it.

Now they were up in space, everything became weightless. There was no up or down.

Everyone had to get used to floating.

Some of the animals didn't enjoy this.

Neither did Mrs. Noah.

For forty days and forty nights, Noah and his family traveled through space, looking for a new planet. Then, they saw a beautiful blue and green world shining below them. "We'll try there," said Noah.

Ham and Mrs. Noah went ahead in a space probe.

They needed to test the air on the planet to see if it was safe to breathe.

Seven days passed. Everyone waited anxiously
for their return. Then Ham and Mrs. Noah were
back, full of excitement. It was safe to land!

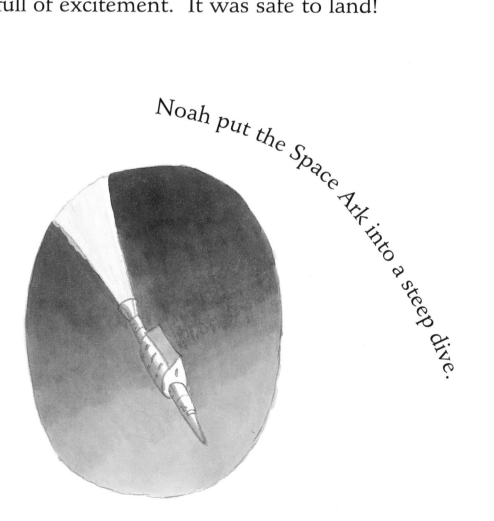

Noah put the Space Ark into a steep dive.

They landed on the planet with a shudder and a bump. When they looked out, they were amazed.

Animals and trees were everywhere, and a huge rainbow shone across the sky. Hannah took a deep breath of fresh air. "It looks like a picture in one of your history books, Grandfather," she said.
"We have found our new home," said Noah.
"And this time, we'll take better care of it."

For Josie—E.C.C.

This edition first published in 1998 by Carolrhoda Books, Inc.
Text copyright © 1997 by Laura Cecil
Illustrations copyright © 1997 by Emma Chichester Clark
First published in the United Kingdom by Hamish Hamilton Ltd, 1997

Carolrhoda Books, Inc., c/o The Lerner Group, 241 First Avenue North, Minneapolis, MN 55401 U.S.A.

LIBRARY OF CONGRESS CATALOGING-IN-PUBLICATION DATA

Cecil, Laura.
Noah and the space ark / by Laura Cecil ; illustrated by Emma Chichester Clark.
p. cm.
Summary: Many years in the future when the Earth has become too polluted to support life, Noah and his family build a space ark and take the animals and plants that are still surviving to search for a new home.
ISBN 1-57505-255-5 (alk. paper)
1. Noah (Biblical figure)—Juvenile fiction. [.1 Noah (Biblical figure)—Fiction. 2. Pollution—Fiction. 3. Animals—Fiction. 4. Science fiction.] I. Chichester Clark, Emma, ill. II. Title.
PZ7.C29975No 1998
[E]—dc21   97–12428

Printed in China by Imago
Bound in the United States of America
1 2 3 4 5 6 - OS - 03 02 01 00 99 98